Spider-Man is on patrol in the city. As he swings along, he sees the streets are a real mess. "How did this happen?" he wonders. "This looks like a job for your friendly neighborhood Spider-Man!"

"It's the Lizard!" Spider-Man shouts. "Wow, how did he get so big! He must be eating his vegetables."

Spider-Man tries to get the Lizard's attention. "Hey big green, what's with the mess?"
But the Lizard ignores him. "Go away, I'm looking for something!"

"That's no way to find something," Spider-Man says. "You're wrecking the place and scaring everyone."

"It's not here!" the Lizard shouts. "I have to find it. I need it quick!"

The Lizard runs off, knocking more things over.
"If the Lizard keeps searching like this," Spider-Man thinks, "people could get hurt!" Luckily, he has an idea.

7

"Hey Lizard," Spider-Man says. "I bet I can find what you're looking for before you do!"
The Lizard is surprised. "No!" he shouts. "You'll just take it!"

Spider-Man lets the Lizard chase him through the city. "Maybe if I tire him out," he thinks, "He'll calm down."

The Lizard tries to grab Spider-Man, but he's too quick. Spider-man swings safely away.

Soon, the Lizard is nowhere to be found.
"Where did he go?" wonders Spider-Man. "Maybe he's on the roof." Spider-Man climbs up to find out.

Suddenly, the Lizard breaks through the wall! **"No! It's mine!"** he shouts. It looks like Spider-Man is in trouble!

But then, the Lizard stops suddenly. "Oh no!" he cries, "I'm stuck!"

"Now, what's all this about, Lizard?" Spider-Man asks. The Lizard looks sad. "I made a machine to make things shrink and grow. I made myself really big, but I now want to make myself regular-sized again."

"Where did you have it last?" Spider-Man asks. The Lizard thinks hard. "I know! The machine is red so I put it down near a red building. Will you help me find it please?"

"See? It wasn't so hard to ask for help," Spider-Man says. "I'll help you, but you
  need to promise to clean up the mess you made."
"Okay," the Lizard says. "I promise to clean it up!"

"A weird red machine? Hey, I think I saw it someplace," **VROOOM!** Spider-Man drives off on his stunt cycle to look.

"But where? There are a lot of red buildings in town." Spider-Man thinks.
"I wonder if any of my treasure-hunting reader friends have found it already?"

Spider-Man searches the city carefully. It's a big job but he promised to help. After looking almost everywhere, Spider-Man finally finds the Shrink Ray machine!

"I found it!" Spider-Man says, "Good thing I took my time. That machine was hard to find."

Spider-Man turns on the shrink ray. **WOOWOOWOOWOO!** The Lizard gets smaller and smaller. "I'm my regular size again!" he says. "Thanks, Spider-Man!"

As promised, the Lizard starts cleaning up the city. Spider-Man and the other people help out. "All is well that ends well. Spider-Man says, I hope you've learned something from this."

"I sure have, Spider-Man. I'll be calm and careful from here on —"
The Lizard suddenly looks worried. "Wait a minute. **Where did my broom go?**"

"I can't clean up this mess without my broom! I gotta find it!"
The Lizard runs down the street, dumping out garbage cans. "Where did it go?"
Spider-Man shrugs. "Here we go again!"

Team up with Spider-Man for your own web-slinging adventures!

SPIDER-MAN STUNTACULAR SPEED LOOP PLAYSET

SPIDER-MAN STUNT CITY PLAYSET

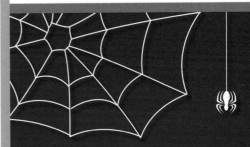

Spider-Man Figure 2 Packs
COLLECT THEM ALL!

Each sold separately.

SPIDER-MAN & DOC OCK

SPIDER-MAN & RHINO

SPIDER-MAN & LIZARD

SPIDER-MAN & GREEN GOBLIN